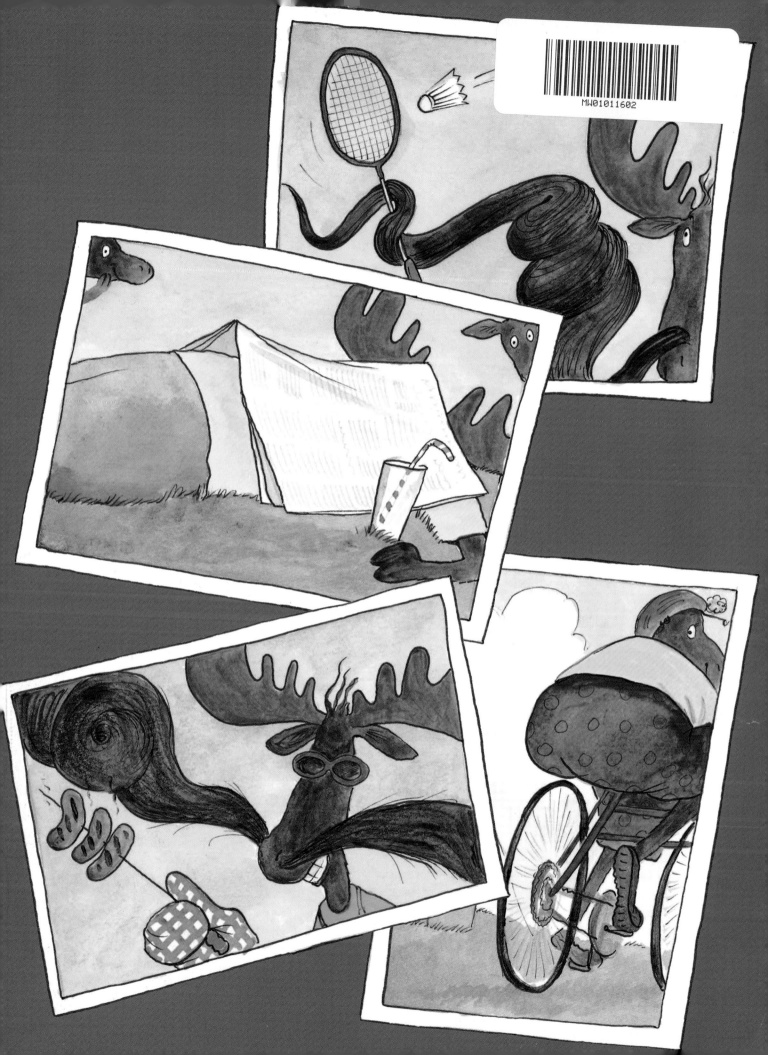

Moosekitos
A Moose Family Reunion

Margie Palatini
Illustrated by Henry Cole

HYPERION BOOKS FOR CHILDREN

NEW YORK

Printed in Singapore.
First Edition
3 5 7 9 10 8 6 4 2
This book is set in 16-pt. Meridian, and Improv ICG regular.
Reinforced binding

Library of Congress Cataloging-in-Publication Data on file.
ISBN 0-7868-1955-3

Visit www.hyperionchildrensbooks.com

To my family of "happy campers"
—M.P.

For my pal Windbag, with a big
"How How!" and thanks for the memories!
—H.C.

Moose was feeling a mite melancholy. A bit blue. Sort of sad.

He was missing his big moosey family.

Why, he hadn't seen them in years. Looking at old family photos was almost bringing him to tears.

Moose missed being together. Making memories. Enjoying good times.

He even missed grumpy Uncle Hairy and cousin Curly's bad jokes. Aunt Lerlene's bad cooking.

Moose sighed. Gosh, how he longed to see all the folks.

"My poor down-in-the-
dumps dear," said his darling Mrs.
"There's no need to pine, long, or be lonesome. Let's
plan a party! A reunion and celebration! My love, what
do you say to an old-fashioned family vacation?"

WRONG NUMBER!

A family reunion vacation? How simple.
How easy. **How perfectly perfect!**
Moose calls went out.
North to south, east to west, and all places in between.
From the relatives up in Moosachusetts to the kin
down in Moosissippi. To Mooses in Texas, Montana,
and even south in Alabama. The whole hairy herd
would meet up at their mountain Moose Lodge!

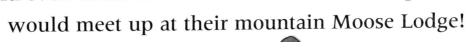

KUM - BA - YA KUM - BA - YA

A big family reunion vacation! Moose's moosetache curled in anticipation.

He planned three-legged races for the very first day. Silly songs for the next. He scheduled swimming. And sunning. Tanning and fanning. Boating. Floating. Hiking. Biking. Mornings to fish. Time to chat and to dish.

And everyone sleeping under the stars.

"Togetherness," sighed the merry moose. **Positively, perfectly perfect.**

With calendars marked with an X, and watches synchronized to the second, Mooses from coast to coast loaded up cars, packed vans, and stuffed trucks.
Toot. Toot. Honk. Honk. Lots of good-bye waves, and off they went.

Caravans chugged up hills. Slid down dales. Snaked through tunnels. Crossed bridges. Rivers. This way. That way. Left. Right. Left. Left. Right—to the tippy-top of the mountain, and Moose Lodge.

Aunties, uncles, sisters, brothers, each and every cousin piled out to meet and greet. There was lots of moose hugging, cuddling, and kissing. Hand-shaking. Backslapping. Hand clapping. Tears and giggles, too.

It was just as Moose had hoped and planned.

"One big perfectly perfect family reunion!" said Moose, ready with his camera and a click. "All together again! Now, everyone say cheese!"

"Aaa——a-a-a-chooo!"

No. No. That was a sneeze.

Moose looked at his darling wife. Her eyes were suddenly bleary and teary, her nose runny and red. "I tink I'mb allergic," she sniffed. "I'mb going to bed."

Before Moose could refocus, Bucky, Junior, and the rest of the boys grabbed a volleyball and raced off. Sissy and the girls scooted to the beach. Cousins Larry, Moe, and Curly climbed into a canoe and paddled away on the lake. Great Aunt Matilda trailed off to bird-watch, for heaven's sake.

The kin from Montana vamoosed and went for a hike. Great-great-granny toodled off on her bike.

Then the cousins from Texas got ornery and started to squabble. The four sisters from Moosissippi got into a tiff. Uncle Hairy started grumbling and stomped off with a sniff.

"Stop! Wait!" cried Moose, watching them scatter. "What about togetherness?"

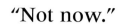

"Not now."

"Maybe later."

"Catch you next time."

"Mind your own beeswax!"

"Go fly a kite."

The family was not playing ball. At least not together.

Moose tried, he really tried to find something they all wanted to do.

It was not simple. It was not easy. And . . . it did not work.

But Moose was still hopeful. He had an idea.

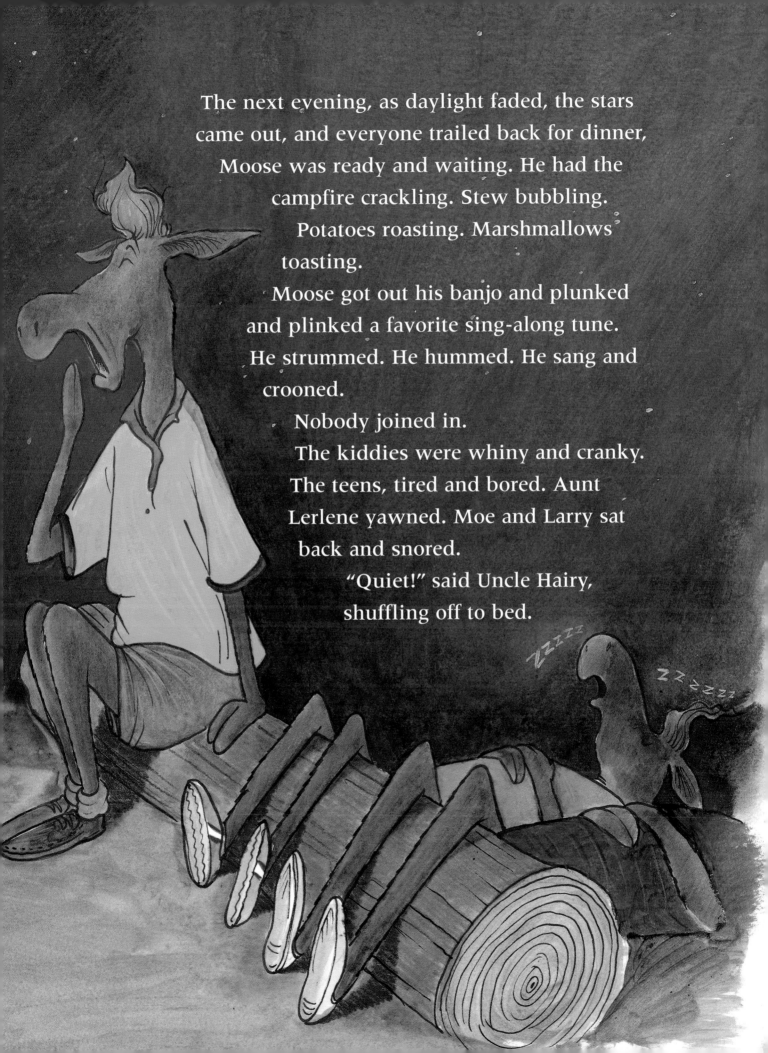

The next evening, as daylight faded, the stars
came out, and everyone trailed back for dinner,
Moose was ready and waiting. He had the
campfire crackling. Stew bubbling.
Potatoes roasting. Marshmallows
toasting.
Moose got out his banjo and plunked
and plinked a favorite sing-along tune.
He strummed. He hummed. He sang and
crooned.
Nobody joined in.
The kiddies were whiny and cranky.
The teens, tired and bored. Aunt
Lerlene yawned. Moe and Larry sat
back and snored.
"Quiet!" said Uncle Hairy,
shuffling off to bed.

"But what about family togetherness?" Moose sighed, sadly eating a s'more all by his lonesome.

As the last campfire flames flickered, the only sound Moose heard was a *ribbet* solo.

And then from
somewhere in the dark . . .

In the quiet . . . came a *b-b-b-buzz*.

Then a *nhiih*. And a *nheeh*.

And a *nheeehnhiiizzhn*.

"Ouch! Ooooo! EEEEeeeee!
EEeeee! Oooooo! Ouch!"

SLAP. SMACK. SLAP. SMACK.
SCRATCH. SCRATCH. SCRATCH.

"Land sakes!
It's moosekitos!" cried the
Moosissippi aunties, wailing
with alarm.

"Blasted buggy
biters!" shouted Uncle
Tex in the middle of a
swarm.

SLAP. SLAP. SMACK.
SMACK. SCRATCH.
ITCH. SCRATCH.

"Help! Moosekitos!" yelled the boys
as they tumbled off their cots.
"Help! Moosekitos!" cried the girls,
covered with bumpy pink polka dots.

"Do something, my darling!" said Mrs. Moose as she scratched between two *achoos*.

But Moose pondered, wondered, worried . . . what could he really do?

Then suddenly, he froze. One of the biggest moosekitos had landed right on his nose!

Moose gulped and went eye to eye with the big buzzer.

They glared. They stared. Who would blink first?

And then Moose grinned and smiled. He didn't swat, smack, or swish, but knew exactly what to do. Moose reached into his knapsack for his tried-and-true—

Moostache Glue!

Moose ordered one and all to take a heaping hoof-ful of the white pasty glop.

Then Tex lassoed some whiskers from the bottom, while the beehived aunties took hold from the top. Herded around in a circle, everyone took a share of moose hair. Why, even Uncle Hairy took part!

And with Moose's orchestration, a little humming,

and some dandy moosey do-si-dos, together they all wove this way. Then that way. Up. Down. Front. And back.

There was no need to worry.

No reason to fret.

Thanks to Moose and his moosetache,
the family now had the world's biggest
moosekito net!

The glued brood was safe, sound, and snug-
gled all around—with Moose smack-dab in the
middle. Oh yes, it was cramped. It was crowded.
And Uncle Hairy's snores were most definitely loud.

But—they were together at last. As close as any family could be.

Moose sighed. It was a **perfectly perfect** reunion. Even if they did itch.

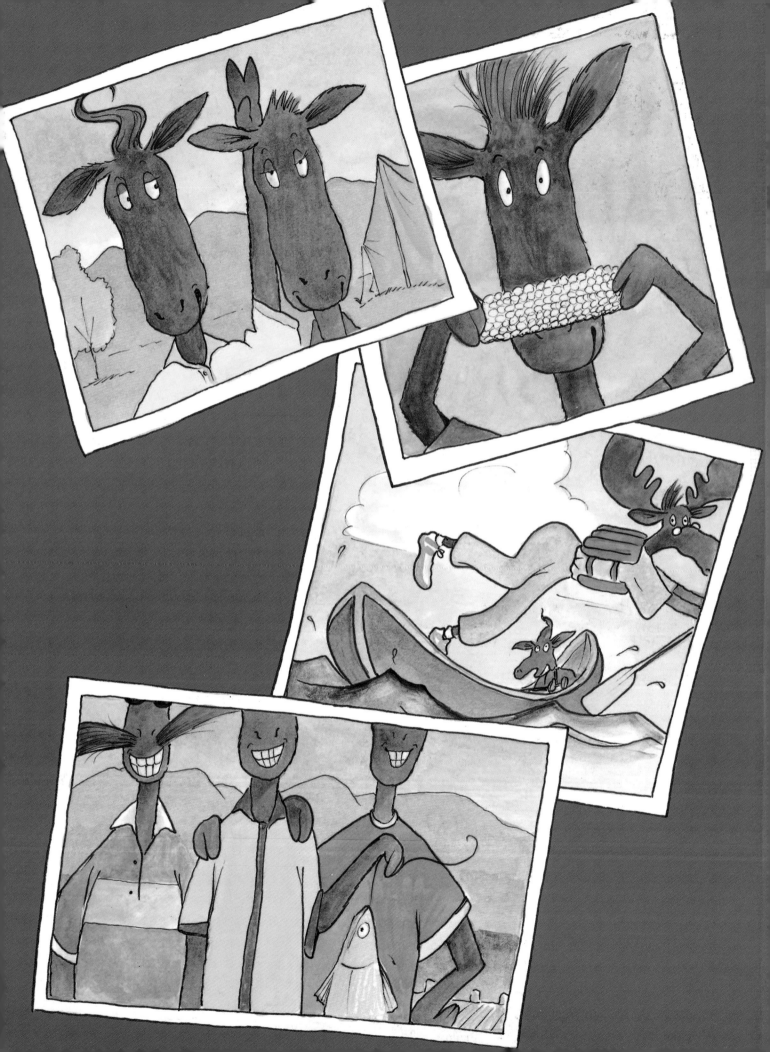